PUZZLE MANOR

Leona's Escape

Forrest West

CONTENTS

LEONA'S LIFE

Leona had always been a fan of games. Her earliest memories were sitting on the couch next to her father, who was playing video games, while she begged to be given a controller despite not knowing how to use it, her curly brown hair haphazardly going in every direction. She played every game she could get ahold of, whether it be a board game, card game, or video game. Leona was always looking for a something new and interesting to occupy her mind, a new challenge for her to overcome.

Leona was fresh out of high school, having graduated top of her class just two months earlier, and was looking for a part time job to make some extra money before heading away for college. She had grown, but still kept her curly brown hair a total mess, and still was obsessed with games. The town of Weston were she lived was small, around four thousand people, and did not have much in terms of jobs. Leona did not want to settle for the construction jobs or maintenance positions available to her. No. She wanted something fun, something exciting, something new.

She tried looking around at the few places in town that were meant for entertainment, but none met her standards. The minigolf course in town was old, worn down, and working there was mostly just cleaning up spilled food from the local kids. There was a bowling alley in town as well, but they were never hiring anybody since the same four people worked there for the last fifteen years. Leona was running out of hope of finding something that fit her playful demeanor and desire for something challenging.

After a day out and about looking for any jobs that matched what she wanted, Leona came home without a single lead. She kicked her shoes off by the door, wandered into the living room, and plopped herself down on the couch.

"No luck today either?" said Nathan, Leona's father, wandering in from the kitchen.

"Nope. I'm starting to think that there is nothing in this town that is any fun. I just want a job that is exciting. I know that it is just a job, but I don't want to feel like I'm wasting my time, you know?" replied Leona without taking her eyes off the television in front of her.

"Well, I might have some good news," Nathan said with a smile on his face.

Leona just noticed he was hiding something behind his back. She looked at him, eyebrow raised pessimistically, doubting her father could actually have found anything worth her time.

"Let me guess. Aunt Brooke has a position open for someone to play bingo down at the retirement home? Or maybe Grandma needs someone to babysit the dog?" She said sarcastically while rolling her eyes before returning to watching her show.

"Not quite as fun as bingo, but I did find this flyer for a new business opening up in town! It seems exactly like the kind of place you've been looking for. Maybe you should give them a call?" Nathan chimed in with a big smirk on his face. He had been hiding a flyer behind his back, which he now excitedly waved at Leona.

She looked at him hesitantly before reaching out and taking the flyer.

"What is this place? Puzzle Manor?" She asked questioningly.

"It is an escape room! You remember that place we went two summers ago? That room where you had to solve a bunch of puzzles to get out? You loved that place! I bet you'd be a great fit for one of those!" Nathan jumped in before Leona could even finish reading the flyer. "What do you think?"

Leona continued to look over the flyer. She had to admit that it did sound interesting. She loved puzzles and did really enjoy the escape room her father had taken her to. Why not? This was the best fit she had found yet, might as well give it a try!

The next day Leona called the number listed on the flyer to ask about getting an interview. It went to voicemail, but the voicemail did mention they had an email where possible applicants should send their resumes. So, she hopped onto her laptop, pulled up her default resume template, quickly typed in what little information she could provide, and emailed that to Puzzle Manor with only a small hope she would hear back.

She checked her email the next morning.

Nothing.

She checked it that evening.

Nothing.

She impatiently checked her email nearly every ten minutes for a week just hoping to hear something back. Even if they had no intention of hiring her, she just wanted to know so she could stop obsessing. Finally, two weeks later, she had given up. Clearly, they had no interest in her. There goes her one chance at a fun job.

Ding Her phone goes off letting her know she has a new voicemail.

"Weird, it didn't even ring," Leona mumbles to herself while pulling out her phone, stopping to admire her hand made green case, covered in goblins. "I don't recognize this number," Then it clicks with her, "Wait, THEY CALLED ME BACK!!!" She yelled while jumping out of the chair she had been sitting in. She landed on the ground with such a loud thud that her father came in looking concerned.

"What? Are you okay? What's happening?!" Nathan asks looking around confused.

"Puzzle Manor called me!" Leona says excitedly while running in circles around the room. "They finally got back to me!"

"What did they say?" Nathan asked excitedly.

Leona stops running around and stares at her father. She pauses, looks down at her phone, and gets a worried look on her face. "I don't know yet. I haven't listened to their message..." Leona whispers with a concerned tone.

"Hello, this is Puzzle Manor calling for Leona. We received your resume and were wondering if you wanted to come in for an interview. We are doing interviews on Wednesday and Thursday starting at one pm. Call us back whenever you get the chance, and we'll figure out what time works best for you. Thanks again for your interest and hope to hear back from you soon," then shuffling can be heard as the manager on the other end tries to hang up the phone.

"Yes! YES, YES, YES!!!" both Leona and Nathan shout joyfully while jumping up and down together.

Leona scheduled her interview for Thursday at two pm.

PUZZLE MANOR

When Leona arrived at the location, she was surprised to see that the business was in fact an actual manor. She was expecting the name Puzzle Manor to be just that, a name. This was not just some regular small town business store front, instead it was an old Victorian house just off the main street into town, with a small path heading up to it and a parking lot outside with room for just five cars. The inside of the building was an interesting mix of the Victorian aesthetic and more modern design. There were large archways left from the original architecture, but the paint and furniture had a much sleeker design. The colors of everything where red, black, or white.

Leona wandered inside and stood by the large black desk that had been placed at the entrance, clearly meant for people to check in at. She waited for a few minutes, expecting someone to come out, but then after a bit decided to sit on the bright red couch placed along the opposing wall. She sat there for a few more minutes, waiting.

Eventually, a woman with short, bright purple hair came out from the back room. She was clearly focused on the clipboard in her hands and did not even notice Leona at first. Leona stood up and walked over to the desk that this woman was now standing behind.

"Hi, I'm Leona. I'm here for an interview," Leona said confidently while holding out her hand. She was doing everything she could to come off as confident as possible, despite being very nervous for her first interview.

The woman looks up, almost seeming surprised, before a look of realization spreads across her face.

"Oh YES! LEONA! I'm soooo glad you made it! I'm just running a little behind, so I'll be right with you dear. Please just sit and relax for a bit," She gestured at the couch Leona had been sitting on before, "By the way my name is Alyssa, it's nice to meet you. I'm the owner and designer here!"

After exchanging a few more pleasantries Leona sat down on the couch and waited while Alyssa shuffled a few more papers around, disappeared into the back room again, and struggled with getting a computer to cooperate with her. After around ten minutes of this Alyssa turned to Leona and let her know that she was finally ready. She led Leona into a side room that looked to be Alyssa's office, and sat down at the desk.

"So. First things first. I have to ask; do you know what an escape room is?" Alyssa asked while looking at her clipboard.

"Yes, I did one with my father a couple years back. I had a great time. We even beat the room with time to spare!" Leona replied eagerly.

"Good! Good. Then I don't have to spend time getting you acquainted with the concept. Perfect! Then in that case let me just go ahead and get right to the main part of this interview. I'm sure you're hardworking, love fun and games, and all that stuff, but I don't really care about finding that out right now. First I have a test for you," Alyssa said while a maniacal smile spread across her face. "I want you to play our escape room".

"Um, okay, that sounds like fun!" Leona replied, somewhat confused.

"It IS fun! I'm sure you'll do great but let me go ahead and break things down for you a bit. Now, normally players would go in as a group and have sixty minutes to solve all the puzzles and complete the room. You will still have sixty minutes so that's no different, but you'll be doing it yourself".

"No problem, I've always been great at puzzles and to be honest when I did the room with my dad, I was basically having to do all the puzzles myself anyways," Leona chuckled.

"Excellent! Well there are a few other things to keep in mind. Normally here at Puzzle Manor we offer unlimited hints for our players to ensure that they have a good time and get to experience all the puzzles, but for this test you only get to use one hint. You still have to get through the room in sixty minutes, and if you can't get through the room then I'm sad to say I won't be hiring you. I want to make sure employees here are of the best quality," Alyssa said with a sort of smugness in her voice.

Leona was a bit surprised by the turn of events. She had been expecting a more traditional interview where she would be asked about her customer service skills and ability to work in a team, maybe a few hypothetical scenarios to see how she would react in certain situations. Instead she is getting challenged to an extra hard version of a game. She was ecstatic.

"I will make sure to not let you down! I'm honestly looking forward to this. I have always loved games, especially when it is a challenge," Leona said enthusiastically.

Alyssa smiled and led Leona out of the office and into the back room. There was a long corridor leading to a door that had been decorated with fake stones and what looked like ancient runes.

"Alright, so let's begin. In this game you are an archeologist who has stumbled across the ancient tomb of a legendary sorcerer, named Duram, and you went in to investigate. When you entered the tomb, the door behind you shut and seems sealed. You must now go forward into the tomb in search of a way out. Are you up to the task? Can you escape from Duram's Tomb?" Alyssa said while smiling, just before breaking out into ominous laughter.

ENTER DURAM'S TOMB

Leona nodded excitedly and headed into the room. Upon entering, it was like she was transported to another world. The walls had been completely covered with grey-blue stone, making it feel as if she had actually walked into an underground cavern. Moss was draped on everything, giving it an old, unkept feel. Even the air felt cooler in the room, as if she was in a cave. There was also music playing throughout the room. Not loud enough to be overwhelming, but enough to enhance the atmosphere. The music was pulsing, almost primal sounding drums, with some kind of flute like instrument playing behind it, sounding similar to a bird call.

The first room Leona entered was rather large. It was essentially a rectangular room, with the door she entered from on one of the shorter walls, with another door across the room and a third door on the wall to her right. In the center of the room was a large stone pedestal. It was circular, but the circle was divided into 5 sections, almost like it was a pie. Each section had a different symbol carved onto it.

Above the door across from Leona, there was a large stone eye carved into the wall with a glass pupil, and above the door she had just entered was an hourglass with minutes marked next to it, showing how much time she had left to complete the room.

Wandering into the room a bit further, Leona noticed there was also a skeleton wearing armor sitting on the floor next to the side door, as well as three shields mounted to the wall next to the door. Underneath the shields was a table with six small chests on it. She headed over to the skeleton and began searching for any kinds of clues. She found an old journal with tales of the daring knight who got trapped in this tomb and never escaped. Within the journal there was also a page of runes translated to English letters.

```
A = ᚠ   B = ᛒ   C = ᛀ   D = ᛞ   E = ᛗ
F = ᚹ   G = ᚷ   H = ᛈ   I = |   J = ⌐
K = ᚴ   L = ᚱ   M = ᛗ   N = ᚦ   O = ᛃ
P = ᚲ   R = ᚱ   S = ᛋ   T = ↑   UV = ᚢ
W = ᚻ   X = ᛉ   Y = ᚫ   Z = ᚤ
```


    She stashed the journal away, assuming it would be of help later, and continued rummaging around the fallen knight. She found hidden beneath the shield of the skeleton knight a strange statue of a fish. Leona stared at the statue, trying to figure out what it could mean, but after looking around the room could not think of anything yet.

"Well, this room is tough right off the start!" Leona said to herself, "I might actually have some trouble here!"

She went closer to the door that was under the stone eye but could not find anything special about it. She could not even find a door handle! Giving up on that door for now, she walked back to the door next to the skeleton to investigate further. Upon closer inspection, Leona noticed that there was a picture of a shield carved into the door.

"Hmm, that's interesting," Leona thought to herself. "I wonder which shield that could be referring to. The knight had a shield, but he came here after the tomb had been made, so I doubt his shield would be the key. Maybe one of those shields on the wall!" Leona couldn't help but smile at the challenge she was facing.

The shields on the wall were round shields, each a different color. One was red with bronze metal, one was brown with silver metal, and one was blue with gold metal. Leona stared at the shields for a bit, but as nothing was obvious to her yet she decided to look at the chests on the table beneath the shields instead. Each chest looked identical on the outside, a traditional brown wood chest like you would see out of any fantasy or pirate story. Inside however, each chest was lined with either blue fabric, red fabric, or left with just the brown wood showing. Each chest also contained a small statue made of either gold, silver, or bronze. The statues were of warriors, all holding various weapons.

Leona stared at the statues and chests for a bit, pondering what they could mean, when she realized something. All of these colors matched the colors of the shields above! The statues were the same colors as the metal on the shields, and the lining of the chests matched the shields themselves. She began placing the statues in the chests that matched the colors of the corresponding shields. She placed the bronze statues in the chests lined with red, she placed the silver statues in the chests left with the brown wood, and she put the gold statues in the chests lined in blue. When she placed the last statue into the correct chest, she heard a click come from the door that had the shield carved into it, and just as she turned to look at the door, it began to rumble and descend into the floor.

Leona stared in awe, amazed by the production value of the room. After the door had descended into the floor, she began to walk towards the opening, only stopping to check how much time she had used. It had been almost five minutes since she entered the room. She felt proud of how fast she solved the first puzzle and after a moment of congratulating herself she proceeded to enter the next room.

DELVING DEEPER

The second room was much different than the first. In fact, it was more of a corridor than a room. It went off both to her right and to her left, curving until she could not see either end of the hallway. On the wall immediately across from the door that Leona had just opened, was an inlet carved into the stone wall, with a small statue of bird. The bird statue was the same size as the fish statue Leona had found earlier, so she assumed they must go together and would come in handy later. She put the bird statue with the fish statue for safe keeping.

Continuing into the hallway, Leona decided to head left first. She walked to the end of the hallway and found an eye carved into the wall, much like the one in the first room. This one also had a glass pupil, but besides this eye there seemed to be nothing on this end of the hallway, so Leona turned around and headed back the other way.

As she walked down the right side of the corridor, Leona began to wonder how big this room actually was. She had solved the first puzzle seemingly quickly, but does that mean there are a lot more puzzles or did she simply solve that puzzle quicker than most? She would simply have to finish the room to find out she supposed.

"But what if I fail? What if I can't beat the room in time? I really do want this job," Leona worried to herself. "No time to dwell on it. I just have to solve all these puzzles and then I won't have to worry!"

Having reached the end of the right side of the hallway, Leona noticed a door way leading into a circular room. The floor had elaborate stone tiles formed into various rings in the round room. To the right of where Leona was standing, there was a second doorway seeming to go further into the tomb. In the center of the room was a strange stone wheel, but when Leona tried turning it, it would not budge. Giving up on the wheel for now, she decided to head through the new doorway.

Looking around the new room she found herself in, she first noticed how many more puzzles there seemed to be in the room. On one wall, directly across from the entrance to the room, there were pictures of various animals carved into the stone, including a bear, pig, owl, wolf, ox, bat, fish, and a deer. Beneath those carvings was some kind of maze full of runes sitting on a stone slab.

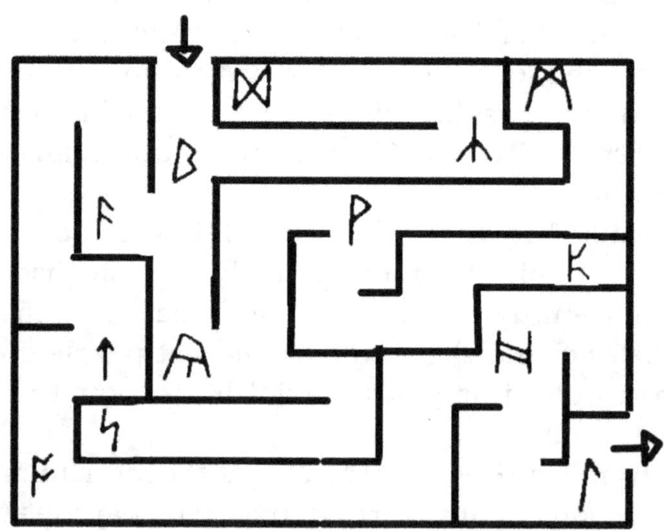

On the right wall was several runes carved into individual stones in the wall, along with a stone slab with some kind of strange code carved into it.

On the left side of the room, there were various weapons scattered across the floor. Against the wall was a simple wooden table with a single drawer next to a weapon rack. Above the table there were also a few places to hang weapons. In the left corner, there was also a door with a large metal lock on it, seemingly needing a key to open.

Looking around this room Leona began to feel a little overwhelmed, becoming more and more aware of the seconds passing by.

"Where do I start? What do I do?" Leona wonders to herself.

Calming herself, Leona decides first to head to the left side and investigate the door. After playing with the lock for a bit she decides that she definitely needs to find the key first and instead begins to investigate the weapons.

"Now what am I supposed to do with these?" she asks herself out loud. "My first guess would be to clean them up I guess?"

She decides to do just that, picking up all the weapons and either putting them on the weapon rack or hanging them on the wall above the table. She hangs two axes on the wall, puts the three swords on the weapon rack, along with a third ax and a bow. She looks at her work and now happy with the result looks around to see if anything has happened.

Nothing.

She tries looking at the weapons to see if there is some secret message.

Nothing.

Frustrated, Leona stares at the weapons, wondering what she did wrong, or if the weapons even matter. She thinks to herself, "What? Are these weapons just here to mess with me and waste my time? Are they just for decoration?"

Just as Leona is reaching her wits end, she hears a voice echo through the room.

"It has been thirty minutes. You're half way through your time dear. Remember you do get one hint if you need it!"

It was Alyssa.

Leona, enjoying the challenge of the room but frustrated with how much time she has wasted, decides it is better to get her one clue now rather than failing the room entirely.

"Alright, I'll go ahead and use my hint now," Leona defeatedly says.

"Check the drawer on the table dear, maybe that can help with your current predicament!" Alyssa's voice chimes in.

Leona stares blankly at the table.

She forgot to check the drawer.

Leona begins laughing, she cannot believe what a silly simple mistake she made. Normally a person would be frustrated by something like this, but Leona just finds it funny. She has always been able to laugh at herself.

Leona opens the drawer and finds a paper with a picture of the weapons on the weapon rack and on the wall. In the picture the bow is hung up and one of the axes on the wall was supposed to be on the weapon rack. She had been so close by pure chance. She puts the weapons in the proper place, and just as she does so, a key drops from a small hole in the ceiling, landing on the table in front of her.

Excited, Leona grabs the key and runs over to the locked door. Using the key that just fell, she is able to undo the large lock on the door, revealing a small closet. Sitting on the shelf in the closet is a statue of a dragon, the same size as the fish and bird statues she found before.

THE TWISTING HALLWAY

With three statues in hand, Leona begins to feel that the end goal of this room is to collect all of the statues. She has to wonder though, what is she supposed to do with these statues? Feeling the need to figure out what to do with the statues, she begins looking around the room. She does not think that it relates to any of the puzzles in this room and decides to head back.

Both the circular room and the long hallways seem to have no use for these statues, so Leona decides the statues must be for something in the first room. Looking around the first room she reminds herself that the only things left in the room that need to be used are the eye above the other door and the large pedestal in the center that has symbols drawn on it.

Staring at the symbols on the pedestal, she begins to have an idea. Leona becomes more and more certain that the statues relate to these symbols.

"These symbols seem like the must represent things. This blue one looks like water, this white one is a cloud, the red is fire, then a green leaf, and a black skull. I bet I need to place the correct statues on each section!" Leona deduces.

She looks at the statues she currently has and decides the clearest one is that the fish belongs on the water section. The second she places the fish statue on the water section, the symbol begins to glow blue! Excitedly she decides where to place the other two statues, ending up placing the dragon on the fire symbol and the bird on the cloud. Both symbols begin to glow in their respective colors!

Progress!

Leona, now knowing what it is that she needs to do, rushes back into the back room that had the weapons in it. On her way out of the first room however, she looked at the timer to see how much time she had left. Twenty-five minutes remaining.

Back in the last room that housed the weapons, she decides to tackle another one of the puzzles. She decides to go straight for the puzzle on the back wall with all the pictures of the animals. She walks over to the wall and touches one of the animal pictures. To her surprise, it lights up! She starts pressing all of the animal pictures and they all light up, but nothing else happens. When she presses them again, the lights turn off.

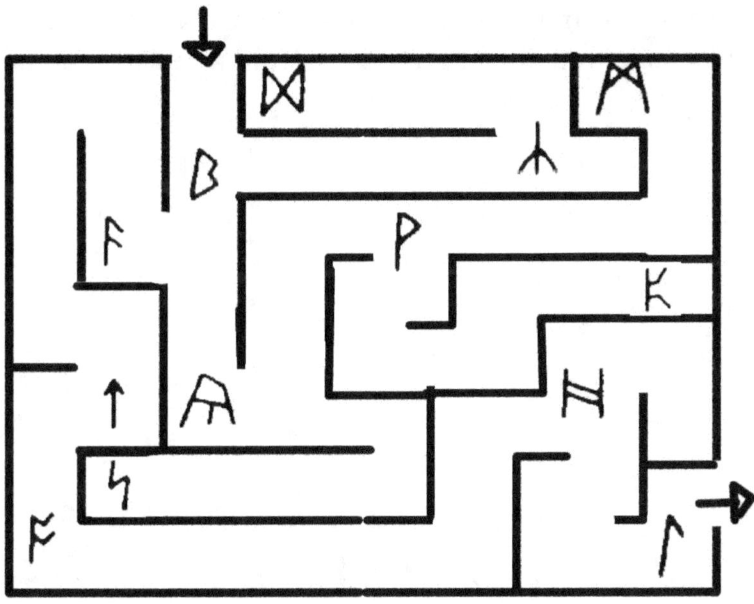

Leona decides that most likely what she needs to do is solve the maze in order to complete the puzzle, so instead of wasting any more time she starts to work on the maze immediately.

After having sat for a little while at the maze making sure she had taken the correct route, Leona began to wonder what solving the maze did. Nothing activated or opened, nothing fell from the ceiling like the key did after the last puzzle. So what was she supposed to do?

"I don't have time for this! Reveal your secrets to me puzzle!" Leona shouted in exasperation.

It was then that she got an idea. There was a secret to the maze! The runes! Enjoying herself thanks to her sudden realization, Leona looked at the runes in the maze, and realized that the path to solve the maze goes through just a few of them. Taking out the journal she had found on the knight earlier, she translates the runes.

A = ᚠ B = ᛒ C = ᚲ D = ᛞ E = ᛗ

F = ᚹ G = ✕ H = ᚦ I = | J =]

K = ᚴ L = ᚱ M = ᛖ N = ᚷ O = ᛟ

P = ᚳ R = ᚱ S = ᛋ T = ↑ UV = ∧

W = ᚻ X = ᛉ Y = ᚬ Z = ᛦ

The runes on the correct path translate to: batowl.

"Batowl? What does that mean? Did I take the wrong path or something?" Leona wondered while looking around the maze.

As she continued to look around trying to find some meaning to batowl, she looked up at the wall covered in animals. She stared at the animals, waiting for something to click in her mind. It was then that she realized she had made another simple mistake. It did not spell batowl, it spelled the words bat and owl! She was supposed to push all the bats and owls! Having realized this, she pressed all the pictures of owls and bats on the wall, and after they all lit up she heard a loud click coming from behind her.

As Leona turned around to see what had activated, she noticed there was now a light shining down on the wheel in the center of the round room. She looked around to see if anything else had happened, but since she did not see anything, she headed towards the wheel.

When she tried to turn the wheel before nothing happened. What about now? What does the wheel do?

She decides to try to turn the wheel, and as she does so she begins to spin. But wait! It is not just her spinning, she is spinning the whole round room, walls and all! As she continues to spin the room the openings where the doors were move with her, revealing a hidden room across from where the weapon room once was. She can now also see the eye that was on the left end of the curved hallway, which seemed meaningless before.

In the new room that was revealed there is a beam of light coming out of the wall, shining towards the center of the round room. Beneath that is a small mirror hanging by a rope.

Walking in, Leona immediately takes the mirror and begins to wonder what she is supposed to do with it.

"Clearly this mirror is important, and so is that light. My guess is they go together, but what do I do with them?" She ponders.

First thing Leona tries is to reflect the light with the mirror back into the hole where the light is coming from.

Nothing happens.

From there she decides to step out of the way and see where the light goes if she does nothing. It just shines across the center of the round room over to the opposite wall. Then, she remembers the stone eye in the hallway! She goes and takes a closer look at the eye and sees the glass pupil that she noticed earlier.

Aha!

Leona heads back into the round room and positions herself so that she can see both the stone eye and the source of the light. She lifts the mirror and positions it so that she is able to redirect the light directly into the glass pupil of the stone eye. As the light hits the glass pupil, there is a rumbling sound and a stone panel beneath the eye begins to sink into the floor, revealing a new statue!

Leona grabs the statue and heads back into the first room. Taking a closer look at the statue she realizes it is a mushroom and decides to put it onto the leaf symbol since it is a plant.

But the symbol does not light up.

"What? Why isn't it working? A mushroom is a plant so it should go on the plant space!" Leona looks at the statue accusingly, as if her logic should somehow change the answer to the puzzle.

She grabs the statue and puts it onto the black skull space instead, and the symbol lights up. At first Leona looks annoyed, but then a look of realization spreads across her face.

'Oooooh, a mushroom is a FUNGUS! Not a PLANT! It helps decompose dead things! I get it! You're a clever one Alyssa, I'll give you that!" she laughs as she starts heading back to the round room, until she notices the timer.

Only ten minutes remaining.

RUNNING OUT OF TIME

Leona is hurrying as fast as she can back to the round room. She cannot believe how little time she has left! The good news is she only needs one more statue, so she must be getting close right?

"But what if there is another room? Is that door in the front the exit or just leading to a final room? What does that eye above the door do? I can't get the light to bounce all the way up there! What am I supposed to do!" Leona worries in a panic.

Realizing that it does her no good to worry about what comes after she gets the last statue, she turns the wheel in the round room to reopen the entrance to the room that had the weapons in it. She heads over to the right wall to tackle what she hopes is the last puzzle.

Standing in front of the wall, Leona stares again at the confusing code on the wall.

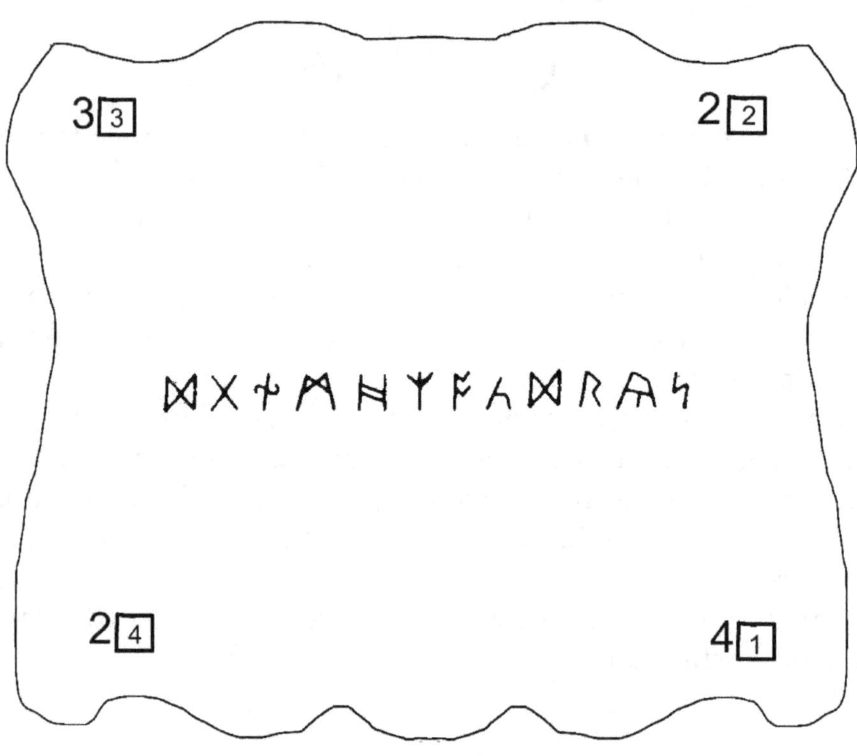

Unsure what it means, she decides to investigate the runes that are carved into the wall near the code. When she touches one, she realizes that they are buttons that can be pressed, just like the animal symbols on the other wall! She is tempted to press all of them again, just like she did with the animal buttons, but she does not want to waste any more of her time. She figures the secret must be in the code and focuses her attention on that.

She does notice that the runes on the code are the same as the runes that she could press, but there is no clear order or pattern to them. Thinking that there might be a hidden message, she takes out her journal that can translate runes to English, but the runes just seem to be nonsense.

"If translating the runes doesn't help me, then what am I supposed to do here? There is no clear pattern, there is no clear message. I just don't get what I'm supposed to be doing!" Leona says in frustration.

"Five minutes left dear!" Alyssa's voice chimes in.

"Well can't I have a hint or something? This puzzle seems impossible!" Leona asks.

"Sorry dear, you already asked for your one hint remember? Best of luck! Four minutes left!" Alyssa replies.

Hopeless, Leona stares at the code. She has always been so good at puzzles, but this one just seems like nonsense to her. She is getting more and more frustrated with each passing second, knowing that she is getting closer and closer to losing. At this point, she isn't even frustrated about failing the test and not getting the job. She just wants to beat this challenge!

That is when she realizes, she should not be getting frustrated, she should be excited about finally coming across a real challenge in this little town!

With renewed enthusiasm, she takes a closer look at the code.

Three minutes remaining.

She looks closer and realizes there are numbers around the outside of the code. What could they mean? There are larger numbers and then smaller numbers in boxes. What do they mean? Is she supposed to do some kind of math? Is it telling her where to look? Is it supposed to have something to do with the position of the runes on the wall? Is it some kind of order?

Order.

The numbers are telling her what order to use to solve the code!

Leona begins frantically trying to figure out how to use these numbers to figure out the order to the code. She hopes that her first guess is correct!

Two minutes remaining.

She sees that the numbers in the boxes go in order. One, two, three, four. The numbers outside of the boxes must be the number of spaces along the code she moves! First rune, four spaces in. She presses the corresponding rune on the wall and it lights up. Second rune, two spaces after the first. She presses that rune on the wall. The third rune is three spaces after that. She presses the rune on the wall.

One minute remaining.

The fourth rune is two more spaces! She presses that rune on the wall.

Suddenly there is a rumbling and the stone that had the code on it begins to slide to the side, revealing a final statue. A flower.

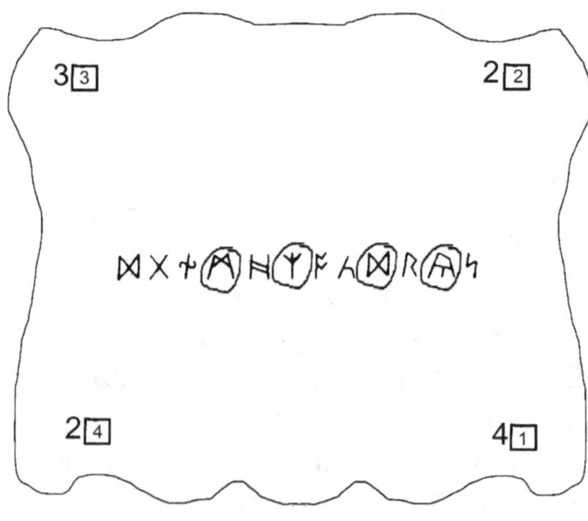

Leona grabs the statue of the flower and rushes into the first room, placing it on the pedestal. The green leaf lights up and the pedestal begins to open. Out of the now open pedestal rises a glowing orb with a beam of light coming out of it. The beam of light shines at the glass pupil in the stone eye located above the one door still closed.

Fifteen seconds remaining.

As the beam of light hits the glass pupil, the door begins to shake and descend into the floor.

On the other side of the door is…

Alyssa, waiting to congratulate Leona on finishing the room!

BACK TO THE
REAL WORLD

"Congratulations my dear!" said Alyssa excitedly. "I'm so glad you managed to finish it, and just in time!"

"I was actually starting to panic there at the end! That was such a challenge, but so much fun!" responded Leona.

After a brief celebration Alyssa led Leona back into her office, where she sat behind her desk once again.

"So, tell me what you thought!" Alyssa asks, paying noticeably more attention than before.

"It was great! There's nothing else like this around here and I really enjoyed the challenge! There were a few moments when I felt a bit silly for missing something, but overall I really enjoyed the experience!" Leona said enthusiastically.

"Well how would you like a job here?" Alyssa asked, smiling.

"Really? REALLY? YOU MEAN IT?!" shouted Leona in reply.

"Of course, dear! Not only did you pass the test, which you are the first so far I might add, but you showed a great deal of wit, persistence, and sense of fun. I think you'd be a great fit here at Puzzle Manor and I'd be happy to have you on board. We are always looking for fun people who can share their passion for escape rooms and create a fun atmosphere. You fit that description perfectly!" Alyssa said with a slight chuckle.

Leona agreed happily, and after filling out some beginning paperwork headed home.

"Dad! I'm home!" Leona shouted as she walked through the door.

Her father Nathan came sliding out of the kitchen. "How'd it go? Good? Bad? I made pie so whether congratulation pie or feel better pie I am prepared!" Her father said anxiously.

Leona, realizing this was the perfect opportunity to mess with her dad, began to look defeated and sad.

"It was horrible! It was nothing like I expected. I show up, wait forever, and then when they finally call me into their office, they said they didn't even want to talk to me!" Leona said dramatically.

"Oh no! Honey! I'm so sorry! That is just—" Nathan began to say.

"And then they made me go and do the escape room and I CRUSHED it and they hired me on the spot!" Leona interrupted with a smug grin across her face.

Leona and her father Nathan hugged and cheered, before wandering into the kitchen to enjoy some congratulation pie. It was apple pie. This was a truly great day.

ABOUT THE AUTHOR

Forrest West

Owner of Quest Puzzles and Escape Rooms, Forrest has always had a passion for puzzles and games. He has dabbled in all sorts of fun activities, but escape rooms have really captivated him and encouraged him to delve into them fully.

Forrest lives in Oregon with his wife Ally, where they enjoy running their business together, playing board games and video games, and going to an escape room whenever they get the chance.